The Ice Factory

PHILIP GROSS

The Ice Factory

ff

faber and faber

LONDON · BOSTON

First published in 1984
by Faber and Faber Limited
3 Queen Square London WC1N 3AU
Filmset by Wilmaset, Birkenhead, Merseyside
Printed in Great Britain by
Whitstable Litho Limited, Whitstable, Kent
All rights reserved

British Library Cataloguing in Publication Data

Gross, Philip
The ice factory.
I. Title
821'.914   PR6057.R/

ISBN 0-571-13217-0

Contents

Acknowledgements

Agenda, Argo, Grand Street (New York), *Listener, Literary Review, New Oxford Magazine, New Poetry* magazine, *New Statesman, Other Poetry, Outposts, Poetry Review, Poetry South East, Stand, South West Review, Vision On, Gregory Awards* anthology 1981/2, *New Poetry 8, New Poetry 9* (Arts Council anthology), *Poetry Matters* (Harry Chambers/Peterloo Poets). Several of these poems, or versions of them, appeared in *Familiars* (Harry Chambers/ Peterloo Poets).

The Ice Factory won first prize in the National Poetry Competition in 1982. A version of *Man and Wife* shared first prize in the Stroud Festival competition in 1980, and *Any Old Iron* won a prize in the Oxford poetry competition in 1981.

Ben's Shed

Clogged webs are slack-strung tennis nets;
    convolvulus, frail horn-gramophones
for bees. Weeds get to work. Leaf shadow frets
the fogged glass. His ironclad mowing-machine,
    tools, flat cap, wellingtons
and, hunchbacked on its nail, his khaki gaberdine

expect him. In this narrow cell, familiar soil-
    smells darken as if underground,
grow tart like old coins or that shred of steel
he took out of swaddling for me once: shrapnel
    the surgeon picked from him, returned
("You shouldn't be alive") as a memento. "Tell

me tell me." He'd no time, "The ground won't wait,
    boy. Nights are drawing in." (August,
bright sun outside.) In his hand he weighed
a clutch of dried corms—hoarded, papery
    shrunk hearts—the past
and future sealed in them; held them to me.

Allies

A sweet smother of gorse,
pods crackling like flame.
Grasshoppers ratcheting. The thrum
of honey-bees recalled the roars
(but distantly) of Flying Fortresses
that cracked the concrete runways
like thin ice. We found no trace

of the airmen, lords of Lucky Strike,
mobbed by the like of us for gum,
except a washed-out YANKS GO HOME.
They went, with razor-blades and Coke
and half the village girls
in tow. The parish in a pique
bulldozed all that was destructible.

Still, their pillboxes squat
in the brambles, low-browed grins
KEEP OUTed and bricked in,
steel hatches rusted shut
(though from beneath the sill
that greenish seep of mud
smelt faintly bestial).

But in a swampy bomb-hole one
slewed backwards, angled
to the sky, door buckled
agape. We hunkered down,
crept crabwise in. And clutched
at the air. Our bearings gone,
we saw each other pitched

at a drunk slant to the floor
and walls, their cocksure verticals
quite unperturbed . . . We scrabbled
out, blinking. Then roared
our bicycles away towards the faint
heat-shimmer where the runway's parallels
dissolved, the vanishing point.

In Another Part of the Wood

a world ends, where a swathe of moonlight
silvers a ten-foot wire. The shadow-
cratered heath beyond is bright
as frost. A few slim birches tiptoe
in among cowled pipes, squat tumuli
with concrete cladding, grilles that hum.
It's here, the future's archaeology.
Not a living soul stirs

                              but kids who come
for the fabulous blackberries, powder-blue
eggs in deserted nests, huge lunar mushrooms,
or on the spongy moss tumps, two by two,
conduct their own experiments.

                                   Hush
hush: two wobbly spooks of steam
twine upwards from their buried vents
and fade apart, like lovers in a dream.

Blind-Worm

High summer. Girl and boy
at play in her father's garden. Hide-and-seek.
   I hid, but where was she?
The minutes, and the laughter, seeped away.
   I stiffened, then stumped back.
      Too late. She was lost to me

      rapt, crouching: "Sssh."
It basked on the crazy paving. "Look." I edged
      in close to stare
at the intricate tiger eyes, the tarnished
   chain mail, the blunt dragon head
      tilted to sip the air,

      her hand, outstretched.
"He sees me with his tongue." It flickered, curled
      to her touch, locked tight
to her thin wrist where the pulse twitched.
   It was curious, cool. She smiled.
      I dreamed that night

      of an abandoned garden, dark
weed-undergrowth. That blank Egyptian stare
      was waiting. Tame,
how tame, said the lipless smile. The black
   switch of the tongue ticked, regular
      as radar, marking time.

Appearances

"What's the boy saying?" Gaunt hand wavering
at me, nails like polished horn (Don't stare,
your uncle's old and not well), signet ring
a gleam on the wasted flesh (And call him Sir),
the long-toothed grin, its awful vacancy . . .

then "Damn you, woman"—brittle, shrill—
"Where are you?" She moved, his iron-grey
shadow, a tight-lipped watchfulness, to still
him with a touch. She swung his chair away
to face the sun, then summoned me. Outside

she softened, "Look, peaches. From grandmother's
time. Or her grandmother's." She smiled,
not at me, "We belong, you see: maids, gardeners,
caretakers, keepers . . . He's like a child,
wilful, fearful, calling in the dark. And who

looks to appearances, but me? No, tell
your mother: there's nothing here for you."
Low hobbled trees, branches splayed parallel
to take the sun; the fruit . . . "He has the few
that ripen. Come." He was famous in the family,

a stranger, scandalously rich, master of everything
beyond our grasp. She eased the one peach patiently
between fingers that grip, grip as if to wring
from the pale downed flesh some common property,
something given, shared, a ghost of tenderness.

Still Life

We bring her apples, a still-life bowl,
their candid waxy gloss untouched,
immaculate. She strains her head away.

Withdrawn to a fierce distance, she eludes
our pity. Her silence is a curtain hushed
around us. We are closeted with her decay

in the stilled, sour-sweetened air.
The window is a picture of unruffled trees,
kempt fields, cows, rooks: "At Close of Day".

It is a pastel pastoral, a nursery frieze,
among the snaps where grown grandchildren smile
in unrelenting brightness from a distant holiday.

Nothing keeps her but a dumb tenacity.
Time is a slow drip, drip: a colourless
fluid ticks into her veins. We back away,

cumbered with grief, and fail, almost, to catch
what she breathes to the wall . . . "Green. Bitter.
Hard as wood. We packed them under hay.

Some rotted. Rats got some. A few,
years later, lifted warm and sweet,
sweeter than you can buy."

Vapourer

A drop of sugar-water, a jam jar on a string
and hush . . . His flashlight pried among the trees,
jiggled and feinted, then was still. The evening

thickened with scents and chilled, ruffling our hair,
as we shrank to one shadow, watched the jam jar swing
spotlit, a moon-faced grin.
                              Conjured from air

they rose: ghost-waltzers, wisps, dissolving in
and out of light, to flirt, a shimmer, there
and gone. Then one was down, grounded and jittering,

ours. Dazzled by sweetness, the frail feathery
scanners fenced. The tinny flitter of a wing
gold-dusted the glass. We muffled its small frenzy,

ran all the way home. In daylight it weighed nothing,
was a husk, a burnt-out fuselage. He staked it tidily
with pins; I thumbed my *Smaller British Moths*, mouthing

a kind of litany: *Buff Tip, Pale Tussock, Vapourer* . . .
"Again, tonight?" No, no. I couldn't name it, something
gone between us, like our breath frosting the night air.

A Ringside Seat

After the tightrope-walker's steely equipoise,
strongmen, cowed famous beasts, a last fanfare,
hey jumbled in. Dwarfed by their own noise
hey stomped and squabbled through the smoky glare,

oud as a playground. The midget's inconsolable boo-hoo.
The boss clown's cackle and bark. I shrank
back, touched cool canvas, and slipped through
nto darkness . . .

        And that bright world sank
behind, a big ship passing. Suddenly adrift,
I stumbled in mud. Nearby, a guttural hum.
A dog dragged at its chain. A baby coughed
and keened. Dark trailers. Washing on a string.
Stale diesel sweat. And I crouched shivering
by a huge wheel hub; tried to imagine home.

The Floating Bridge

Spick frigates, snub black tugs, seabirds
towed upstream by the tide . . .
                                    To, fro,
it nudged athwart the traffic, neither bridge
nor boat nor good dry land. It slabbered
and clanked. I waved. "What makes her go,
Nan?" "Chains." And I saw them, dredged
up, breaking surface, dribbling black weed
and water, gobbled into cogs. Behind,
oil rainbows settled in the grey-green wake
that lapped the slipway. Mother waved
from midstream, once. Nan took my hand,
clumsy-affectionate, "If them chains broke,
Cornwall'd float away."

                          "The boy won't sleep,"
Mother was at the bedside; at her back,
Nan's voice, accusing, ". . . wouldn't eat all day."
My dumb clinch eased to sobbing, then a deep-
sea swell of weariness. "Now they can break,"
I muttered, "Now. Please."

                          floating away.

The Musical Cottage

An endless Sunday. In the attic room
the solitary child sits. The tune
deliberates each note, each stepping-stone
across depths of silence. From the trim

toy chalet two unchanging faces stare,
a mother and father in separate windows,
weather-people. He sees more than he knows
as he hinges the roof back on the whirr

and tick of cogs, precise machineries
circling on themselves, clinched and
slowing. As "Edelweiss" grows hesitant
he shuts his eyes, wonders "Where *is*

the music?" Elsewhere. He can catch
only the after-trace, the bright splash
dissolving into ripples where the fish
has gone: beyond him, or too close to touch.

The final note hangs frozen at the lip
of being.
   Thirty years.
     It will not drop.

Any Old Iron

The last horse in the city bows her head
with a tumbril of scrap: valve, piston, stopped

hearts of lost machines, clogged arteries,
pipes crusted like Armada cannon. He

bobs to the grandfather-clock clop, eyes
closed, reverent. The mantra that he brays

is the blurt of a conch, one strangulated vowel,
no earthly language. He follows an invisible

dyspeptic glutton god, whose furnace door
slams open like an accusation, a jeer

of light, and stares, devours. The hoard
goes rattling into a white-hot-throated roar,

impartial, bottomless.
                    And is reborn, new-forged.
Flows from the shop floor in a glittering cortège.

The Stadium

A phosphorus white glare
behind the housetops. Out of yards
and ginnels, shadows flowed
together, past my window. Flare

of a match in cupped hands,
embers bobbing. Dark designs.
SPEEDWAY TONIGHT: I heard
the tetchy whoops and whines

of starved machines I never saw.
Next day the track was scribbled,
rucked; the grass here dulled
with dust, there parched to straw;

the corrugated shed (GRANDSTAND
1s 6d) patched with a sign
for Whiffs, a platform on a soon-
to-be-disused branch line.

Chip papers, fag ends, emptiness
with a sweet scorched smell.
And silence? No, a subtle
niggling in my ear, a tinnitus . . .

grasshoppers, coming out like stars
till the whole field thrilled
with brittle simmering applause
. . . abruptly stilled.

"Oy!" Cinders crunched: an oily
grinning giant with a jerrycan,
"Lost summat, boy?"
I up and ran.

The Site of the Crystal Palace

A weed-mobbed terrace; plinths
deserted; an imperial symmetry
partitioned, gone to various bidders.
Down the clogged ghost-promenades

he sees like yesterday, only clearer . . .
Girders wincing, staggering in white glare,
the factory-forged dream, that ordered
brilliance, stove in and shrivelling

to mere recorded fact. More real,
his mother's apron, dabbing smoke-
sting back; her grimed ordinary face,
tired then, lost thirty years now,

but flare-lit that night, immutable.

The Curator's Tale

Where do they come from, or go, these few
a rainy afternoon blows in to share
the stillness of stuffed animals (the kingfisher's
crackling spark, earthed here, is simply blue;
the salmon gapes, embedded stupidly in air)?

Case after case reflects them loitering among
wombat, echidna, axolotl, pygmy shrew;
the Galapagos tortoise, turned to stone
after a lifetime practising; the buttock-faced dugong
that sailors, rank with grog and solitude

took for a mermaid. "That's the stuff
(my little joke) that dreams are made on."
No one smirks. Ah, well. These shrugged-off
species are my stock-in-trade. Yet if
he (facing the Irish Elk) would turn

and speak, and she (by the dusty clutter
of "Fox Cubs at Play") would startle, and respond,
I'd throw the cases open, goldfinches
flirt up in a charm, the grizzled otter
splash clean through the perspex of its pond.

Snail Paces

As I pry beneath crumbling bricks they come
to light, pale embryos unfolding. Slim
  wands question space,

touch-tentative. They lift small frills
to glide and teeter, balancing their shells
  like the family china.
                      Or brace

on the hawser of themselves; the load stirs
and follows like a shadow. Each shoulders
  his small world like a sack.

and strains towards his half-an-inch horizon.
We are less to them than clouds across the sun.
  Beneath the thrush's block

we find them threshed out, littering our grass,
mute violated husks. Bend closer . . . Pass
  down empty corridors,

intimate windings, moulded by the sheer
day-in-day-out of flesh. Mother-of-pearled,
  the inner chamber of the ear.

Crab

Shifty, side-skittling, he's on the run,
    the Scissor Man,
with his antique weapons, his stage-wrestler's pose.

And cornered . . . Cocked, grappling his load
    of menace. Eyes
at the battle-slit, glistening. And afraid,

yes, rigid, in his frightful uniform, my tuppenny
    ha'penny samurai . . .

He squats. Shimmies the quicksand. Melts away.

Facing the Sea

Low tide and winter. Windows full of Vacancies
outface the empty shingle. Miles of esplanade
whose windy shelters bear scars, elegies

to last year's lusts, lost causes, relegated teams.
The hard boys slouch outside the boarded-up arcade
like ghosts of Bank Holidays past, uneasy dreams.

Nothing awaits them, except time. The air
they breathe is bitter, their radios a thin
irritable whine. They neither speak nor stir

as two intruders inch across their afternoon,
old man and boy. Their stare prickling his skin,
the boy stiffens. Oh to be someone else, and soon,

he chafes. To outgrow this half life. To be free
of kindnesses, comforts, tacky threads that bind
him to an out-of-season childhood.
                            ". . . History?"

the old man rambles. His eyes crease but never blink,
as if scanning the sea, as if he were not blind.
". . . Too grand a gent to visit *here*. Or so we think.

At your age I'd crossed three frontiers, left behind
all but what wouldn't leave *me*—a long memory
and a Litvak name. Two burdens, no? You're kind,

despite yourself. You want, and fear, to be alone.
But it goes so quickly, though you won't agree . . ."
The waves' dull rant goes on, stones grind on stone,

march, countermarch. He pauses, as the noise
discloses a far resonance: *"Papa, they hate
us. Why?"*

Lost in the roaring.

But the boy's

grip tightens, pulls. ". . . They smell our fear.
Look at the sea." Behind them both, these shadows wait,
hands idle, toying with a laugh, a stone, a jeer.

The October People

. . . At last, hunger and weariness wore out our fear.
We crept from the forest, found a track, and so
came to the village called October. Blown seeds of war,
we were wretched, ragged. Still, they turned to hear
as if expecting us. Their dialect moved close and slow
around us. Yes, there were soldiers, weeks before,

see there, the flag they left . . . It guttered brown
in the wet wind. Took what they could, promised a new
world, said the farm-wife, bringing to the shed
thin broth in an iron bowl. We huddled down
in rough hay-sweetness. "In the morning, you
must go." "And you?" "We bake black bread,

stack wood, salt beef, bury our savings deep . . ."
The oil wick sputtered. "After, we repair
the damage. Bitter? As well blame
the leaves for falling." Falling into sleep
I dreamed of leaves, of smoky pyres that flare
against the dark, brighter as wind beats on the flame.

Stations

Each country was a station, more or less the same
—clamour in darkness, brilliant shrieks of steam
ballooning into gloomy arches. Everyone was strange,
the fat man huffed and comical, bleating as in a dream
"My bags. Where am I?" Sometimes uniforms would
     change.
Prague . . . Vienna . . . Paris . . . Europe was a game

they should be winning, surely? Town by town, hotels
grew smaller, hosts smiled less, fewer bells rang.
The plumbing was louder, windows smaller to the sky,
back alleys closer, with sunk yards like dried-up wells
where servants clattered, quarrelled and, mysteriously,
     sang.
His parents grew difficult, not explaining why

when letters came, she cried, and later cried again
when the letters stopped. He stood at a kiosk jostling
among dissonant voices, jowled sour-smelling men,
for a paper Father glanced at, then threw down (rain
speckling the page, the dark stain slowly blossoming,
blotting faces, ranks of print . . .). More often then

there were voices raised outside the room, or had he
     dreamed
that? Father and Mother. Le patron and Father. "Please,
please." And there was Mother, bending close, her hand
steadying him, or herself: "Listen. You must understand.
Now we have nothing . . ." And at once, it seemed,
another station: they were struggling trunks (could these

[30]

e "nothing"?) into battlemented piles. Now to play,
Look at me. I'm king . . ." He faltered as he saw
undreds encamped around him, like the tribes of Israel.
Iobody turned. Then a shadow and a roar
f power reined in, steel shrilling on the rail.
he crowd broke round and over him, swept him away.

The Displaced Persons Camp

Lean vigilant faces, sleepless eyes,
look up. They sit like children grown
unnaturally, cramped into desks in rows,
and submit to the language of strangers, stern
new ordering of tenses: *is, was,*

will be. "Repeat now, after me." Each voice
lifts towards clarity, and breaks: waves
on a north shore, a dull bafflement of loss.
"The subtler points, *should, might have been,*
will come, in time." The class dismissed,

they are free to sit, or pace the bare
perimeter. Willowherb flares from the dust.
It is neither peace nor war. Beyond the wire
in wide fields, two boys and a dog
race after their own cries. And stop. And stare.

The Victory Dance

The Village Hall in glad rags. The St Juliot
Swing Combo: "Take your partners, please . . .
(three girls to each man). And let's not forget
our foreign guests . . ."

                    The refugees,
brought from the Camp, clumped round the stove
or drank themselves to tears. But he . . .
That slight stiff bow. He clicked his heels.
"Permit me the pleasure." (Imagine, mother. *Me*.)
He danced like an officer. Yet when the band
came fumbling to a halt, I dared a glance
and caught him lost for words, yes, shy.

Not like that tea-time. The greataunts
closed ranks on the settee, the Three Monkeys
—Pru's puddle glasses; Dot's hand cupped
to her bad ear; Vi's nice inquisition, carefully
enunciated, as if to a child. The tea unsupped.
He was . . . correct: "Madam, I comprehend.
But cannot, as you say, *go home*."

Then Jack was demobbed, full of beer
and battles, thumping "I don't give a damn
what *kind* of foreigner . . ." I was afraid.
By night, voices pitched from the Quarrymen's
Arms, hard laughter.

                How could we have stayed?

And yet . . .

A white-walled hut. The Chaplain's
gruff brusque blessing. A Best Man
who spoke no English. I thought of you,
and a church awash with hymns and flowers.
("You must learn," he said, "you too,
about leavings behind.")

That night,
the only guests in the hotel, we ate
in silence, cutlery chinking on our plates,
the landlady vigilant. Then we flung out
past curtained terraces on to the Prom,
the street lamps smoking with blown spray.
I huddled close, thinking "Soon it must
be easier. We'll know what to say."

I lie awake. Rain chafes the window.
Mother, he sleeps huddled, deep,
but has such dreams. What can I do?
He speaks a foreign language in his sleep.

The Gift

Clogged under cinders, nettles, waste
it could have been a meteorite
or an old potato. But the mud crust cracked
and flaked away, and look,

it's a perfect ovoid, pearl-
iridescent, seamless,
an immaculate earth-shell.
I raise it to you like cut glass.

And there's an ocean in it. Feel the stir
and fall, the tides taut, quivering,
alive. The air
around us has a salt spray-sting

while deep, safe as a sunken galleon
a dim speck quickens,
hunches, shuffling its cells
like an old man playing patience.

A scroll we cannot read yet, it unfurls
itself, a dark map-labyrinth
filling with dawn. Spark trails
open to thoroughfares, transparent

cities like sleeping hives grow gold-
opaque and audible. Dogs bark.
The traffic starts up like an iron waterfall
and people rise, as we do. Take

this, love, this curious weight
on us. It wants to live.
It seeks us out, says *give
me*. And we give, we give.

First Encounter

Abstract and intimate, circling in a void,
you closed on us. The bubble of our world
warped, quivered. You were not to be denied.
A flicker of static, of morse: yes, yes.
A blip on a dark screen, homing. I can't tell
who called, who answered: you or us.
Or gravity, a dumb inevitable fall,
your lit speck skating over emptiness,

irrupting here, in a dazzling antiseptic cell
with dark before and after.
                            "It's a girl",
this lean survivor, streaked with blood and foam.
Now we must wash you into human form,
that venerable head, webbed vellum, purple-
muddied map of a fabulous country, pulsing.

Post Natal

Adrift, and dazed with sleeplessness . . .
    That cry,
needle-thin, frail, pitiless,
   reels me in. Fed, he
     sleeps; I
push back the curtains on a world of time
   grown strange to me.
A milky slick of smoke hangs low
above empty gardens; only sky
   moves, glacially slow.
    He stirs.
   In our warm lit room,
our honeyed cell, I am calm and numb
as if consoled in mourning, but for whom?
    Friends come
tender and hesitant, eyes bright, bearing flowers.

Geminus

Two angels on a pinhead . . . We had everything
in common. We conversed in the original
tongue: one blood, two heartbeats whispering.
We were perfect. We were bound to fall

in time. No elbow-room! I struggled free,
the born survivor. You were too late, too slow,
hunched in on silence. I thrived single-mindedly.
When I was "old enough to know",

they told me about you. What pale child
stared from the mirror on my wall that night?
I knew you, and you me, for you half-smiled
as if shy or blind from too much darkness. One
hand felt towards me, your left to my right:

recoiled, stung by the cold glass in between.

Ignis Fatuus
B.W.R. 1890–1976

Hush now . . .
                    Gone without peace or dignity,
fuddled, muttering, neither here nor there.
Sour difficult aunt few liked or saw
except from duty, I approach you carefully

as if at a touch your special loneliness
might cling, that scent of lavender and ashes
round you like a shifting mist with voices
scolding, daylight fading, *ignis fatuus.*

"This hotel's full of fools . . . And tell
them, it's too hot, the flowers die . . .
There's a nigger at the window watching me . . .
I'm afraid, my dear . . . Shameful, shameful . . .

Take me home now." Veils of librium
to swaddle you. And lastly, in a barred
cot, to be laid out, scrawny as a child,
by the night nurse, a tall bored Nigerian

—an irony that's lost on you.
The words go round. One twist, and look,
it's like eternity, a Möbius strip (a trick
with paper, Bess, the least I can do).

A Plague of Jellyfish

One morning the sea blossomed with them, pale *fleurs du mal*
the Gulf Stream shunted into our too-perfect bay.
They curdled in the waves
and blotched the sand. We mourned the spoiled day
by bickering, then sulked, gazed from the harbour wall . . .

Slow-flouncing, rippling, with movements hardly more
than a tremor of light they massed, small fantasies
in see-through lace
tricked out with poison-hair, the sea's
vague figments, flotsam hushed towards the shore,

threats, promises . . . You reached out, drew us tight
together as that sightless unrelenting stare
surrounded us, mauve-veined
irises flexing as if brought to bear
on unfamiliar distances, our shifts of dark and light.

Love in the Conservatory

It keeps its secrets in a public place,
this cage cobwebbed with winter sun.
Limp gestures, wrought in iron, grace
a prospect of decline. For us who come
to be alone, the door sighs, time waits
among lush forcings of a late imperium.

And the heat! Pale liver-spotted fish
yearn up to their reflections, sip a kiss.
Can we do better? But you're far
away, your fingertips tracing the cicatrice
on smooth bark, name-tagged. *"Mastersonia.*
Who . . ?" The punkah leaves above us stir . . .

"Write . . . But my hands tremble, the page is wet.
    Fever. The night
beasts prowl and call. Or more-than-tropical
    blooms flaunt and fall
before my eyes. Sketch, annotate: lonely
    love's-labours of taxonomy

to ship home (home!) one perfect specimen I dream
    may take my name
in ritual Latin. Thus do I approach the high
    cool vault of history
—in a small way, glass in hand to magnify
    creation, on my hands and knees."

The sunlight empties from our day. We gaze,
apart, through wan ghosts of ourselves, to where
a newspaper lifts and drags across a bald parterre.
A sail, a tattered parasol. Beyond the trees,
the traffic . . . Constant dull insurgency,
the mutterings-in-sleep of distant wars.

Passages from Africa

(North, the Harmattan rasps. Clenching your eyes
    against blown grit, you watch for news
no longer new, from "home" you'd barely recognize.
Now the village boys come whooping, raising dust,
    "A letter, Ma. From England.
Is it from the Queen?")

                  I take on trust
your scorched bush, your savannah skies. What's real
    is thin scribbled paper that I piece
together, searching. Are you there? I feel
the miles between us, the dumb bulge of Africa
    swollen on emptiness that grows,
Sahara, spreading like a slow amnesia.
Herds parch, tracks dwindle, living land
    is ceded, year by year,
pasture to thorn scrub, then to sand . . .

              No, more our scale
    and nearer home, remember
Enodoc's granite chapel, swallowed by a whale
of a dune; whose parson, lowered through
    a hole stove in the roof,
preached to the darkness as if every pew
was aquiver with piety. Not to leave unsaid
    the proper words, that's something.
Come. The cool sand crumples to your tread,
the sea wind stiffens to a shore swept bare,
    hissing the marram, scudding
mist and gulls inland. And this is where
we meet (but when?): a point equally remote
    from your "real world" and mine,
but close, as close as . . .

                    "Speed, Bonny Boat . . ."
Remember that? Your sweet cracked lullaby
   in my four-year-old night
hushed me away. ". . . Over the Sea to Sky . . ."
I lived in a world uncluttered by geography.
   Not the meaning but the sense
of the words beguiled, enfolded me
in distances and whispers, like the sound of rain.
   And now you're over so much more
than sea, listen: it's your song I sing again,
again . . .

        ("Six weeks?" The Postal Agent smiles
           and shrugs. "Madam, you're not
        in Oxbridge Circus now. Two hundred miles
        up country. It takes time.")

                    . . . This empty shell
   of words returns the song to you—
though a cupped hand or tin can would do as well—
"the sea" . . .

           ("The old men," you write, "are gruff
              and chary. Children stare
           frankly from doorways. The women are kind enough
           and chide me gently for my botched Yoruba.
              Last night I asked Ipe
           about the drums. "It's nothing, Ma.
           Nothing to a white lady like you." And then
              that flick-down of the eyes,
           a courteous, final *no*.")

            . . . the sea that men
and wives of Port Quin, Boscastle, Porthissick,
   that scattered fisher-commonwealth,
heard, night and day. Listen. The same Atlantic
parted and connected them, and us to them, and me
   to you.
               ("Curfew tonight.
   Trucks, soldiers on the new highway. But I see,
   hear, say nothing. And so, my dear, would you.
      Instead, I hug my radio
   like a child after lights-out, picking through
   static and martial music to the faint genteel
      ennui of the World Service.
   And they've closed the borders.")

                     So the real
world has its entrances. My window shakes, a low
   crumbling roar. In a Wedgwood sky
a DC-10 banks, basks, immaculate and slow
—a slick fish, belly glittering in the sun
   full of wealth and promises.
It'll score your sky before I've half begun
to write. "If the Good Lord meant our words to fly
   He'd have given them wings."
Perhaps he did.
             Perhaps we can.
                   I'll try.

Croydon 1983

Lullaby
Isles of Scilly

The drowned land in the west.
Remember. Islands that were hills.
   Our boat's shadow slides
above granite parishes, hearth walls,
   acres dissolving into mist

   and "Look" you're agog. A grey
dappled head breaks surface, then two, three,
   all the inhabitants. They stare
with old eyes, as if it were their memory
   we pass through, spray-

   drenched, laughing, in a small
boat. ". . . seals!" Our voices drift
   in the slow wake. They
watch us out of sight. Waves lift,
   fall, lift, fall, fall . . .

A Honeymoon

The sea was tame, but he was clumsy, half afraid.
"Like this," I laughed and dived, slipped through
to a world without walls, my secret smoky-blue
basement. The mirrored ceiling swaying overhead

shattered, but silently. Pale waterbaby, eyes
and hair wild, topsy-turvy, groping in a dumb-
show of dismay, he fell to me. The dream
broke as his hand gripped mine; we rose

into sun glare, beach-cries. He was gentle then
a while, our prints fading off concrete, leading in
to the bare cool hotel room.
                              Some evenings still
as I wait for his key in the lock I think of thin
blue curtains rippling shut, the sudden chill,
the taste of salt, blue shadows mottling our skin.

Beside the Reservoir

A surface still as marble. Drystone masonry
runs straight in, under. There is no other shore
but a thin brilliance of mist. One tree
stoops, waist-deep. At the small thud of a door

the gulls flush upwards briefly. By the car
two figures stand as if breath-taken. Once
they would have talked, talked, troubling to share
this luminous distance. Now, he points

to bird-flecks drifting far out: a precarious
species, winter visitors. She takes his arm,
keeps company, through certain silences
accepted like the need for water, for the drowned farm.

Man and Wife

Jesse

Greatgrandfather, stiff as a parson you
command my presence. Stern proprieties
buttress you, you them. A family, a farm,
a church, a constitution, all
the hard-won hills around you stand

because you do, upright. You must wonder who
this stranger is: what kind of man
never sat at a long oak table, saying grace
over hushed heads, carving knife in hand
with the beef blood on it;

what kind of man never learned through the skin
the leather testament, the print of things
beyond question: belt strap, Ten Commandments;
what kind of man, embarrassed to set his
the last name in your family Bible.

Sons after sons, grown small
before you, felt your great hand raised
like the rainclouds over Cornwall,
tablets of the Law. Old man,
the shadows that you cast

close round you now. Your hands
hang empty. Memories of the soil
you loved and mastered leak
through your fingers. Reach
to me, stranger.
                              And I touch

n old photograph.
                    Your black-on-white
teps back into hundred-year twilight.
peak. "Alone . . . I worked my own
alvation, with these hands." And she?
'hat pale girl at your side?
                            "Alone."

Susannah

Brought to a hard house young,
o a strong cold man who prayed
ike thunder, hammering dull

ouls to pliant leather. Chill
tony water and a smouldering grate,
he scrubbed slate threshold, the family name,

a bed in a crooked room. The man
tamped his features from you: nine
hildren. With the last you died.

                    *

. . like a shadow into shadows,
                            a new voice
n the choir of silences.
                    Your name, that was his

and your father's,
                    spoken in the empty house,
inks without ripple.
                    What inheritance

[51]

is yours?
          Outside, the vixen's cry
shivers and stills,
                    once only, far away.

Objet Trouvé

Waves smoulder into mist and crumple back
leaving this . . . Gross, unaccountable
among weed and flotsam, dumped: a sack
of sodden hide. Raucous and animal,

the stench confronts us as the wind shifts.
The Atlantic like a wild-haired dotty aunt
embarrasses us with her appalling gifts:
seals, whales, cows. Once, an elephant.

In the museum, bold-hatched lines attest
A Beast Unknown to Science, an ignominious
beached hulk. In their Sunday best,
stout men squared up beside the fabulous

pulp. Years later, most would testify
to the gape ("like Judgement Day") of jaws,
that mad, aggrieved, near-human eye;
how they humped it, six men and a horse,

to a driftwood pyre where far into the night
it smeeched and sputtered. Sleepless, many saw
the embers dwindle, wink out, as a white
mist rose on the tide, consumed the shore.

By Wheal Fortune

A petrified forest
of spoil heaps and stacks.
An engine house
like a busted strongbox.

At my feet the scuffed
earth funnelled
to a ragged throat.
A dry chuckle:

"Bottomless?" A shadow
lengthened beside mine,
". . . Who knows? A rich
lode, though she ran

too deep for us."
He stooped to pick
one grubby nugget
among thousands.
                                        Crack,

the sound skittering,
and I gaped. A glitter-
crusted vug
blinked in the light,

Vug: Cornish miner's word for a cavity
in rock, often lined with crystals.

an opened tomb . . .
"Handsome," he laughed
and tossed it clean
into the open shaft

". . . Fool's gold!"
It glinted, fell
without splash or echo,
may be falling still.

Tin Workings, Dartmoor

Wet in all weathers, never warm . . .

A smoky peat stack, boulder walls
thick as your back. Days, years,
they scratched through streams until arthritis bit
to the bone and joints locked tight.

Half a day's journey down a straight stone track.
The village windows watched
these grey horizon-men, their slow
moor ponies bringing down the ore.

A hush at the inn.
They drank, each man
five years aged since they came last year.

Stones among heather, heather among the stones.
Walls gone, their lintels slumped
like drunks in the rubble. Here they ate,
sat on the worst days, slept in rows

and left no messages. Their silence,
standing water furred
by wind, stills for a moment, clears,
gives up nothing but reflections.

The Bone Ship

Carved by
Napoleonic prisoners-of-war
in Dartmoor

Web-traced with blood (marks of the dead,
the felled meat), clouts of bone

whittle to ivory. Bulkhead, stanchion
and spar, a keel ribbed like a bird:

rough hands recall each detail crisp as ice
till she rises again, cambers, rigging braced,

to no swell, and the bowsprit pries
into emptiness, a blind man's wand.

The years slammed shut behind them. Wind
chanking the prison bell. Through bleached

bare decks shadows detach themselves and come
and come towards us, empty hands outstretched.

The Ice Factory

"Not a great deal is known about this
minor industry, which appears to have
had a short life . . ."—Helen Harris,
The Industrial Archaeology of Dartmoor

A hush like a shut Bible. Father: "Grace
will wait . . ." The latch clacks. Our stare
lifts from our cold meat, from the empty place
to the door, and cousin Joseph. His chair
grates on the floor, and Father: "*Now*
let us pray . . ."
             Who knew him? Slow
to speak or laugh, slow at the plough,
some kind of fool, they said. I'd go
to fetch him in from the topmost field:
"This place don't give us nothing free
but rain. So Father says."
                   He smiled.

November: bitter drizzle. He
went up the hillside as the cloud came down.
December: snow penned us behind doors.
The first clear morning, we'd see thin
tracks, wavering slightly, up into the moor.
In March, I followed. Jumbled stone
in a windy hollow; black peat-water riffling;
a turf-wadded hut. "You've come alone?"
He prised the door, "Then look." Nothing,
I saw nothing, or a glistening black, before
the ice-cold took my breath. His chill
smile: "Things aren't always where
they're needed. Are we, girl?"

                        April,
he was gone. Was seen, halfway to town,
cart lumbering under bales of moss and straw,
steaming and dripping. "Taking water down,"
they laughed, "Thought that's what river's for."
Then nothing. Though the horse was found
by the docks where the tall ships come. All year
they traded stories—"mad", "enlisted", "drowned"
—and tell them still for any stranger's beer
since the farm's gone back to moor.
                                    And now
this flimsy envelope: *New York*. Inside,
"My father would have wished . . ."
                              He was rich, somehow.
Had grandsons. Mentioned me before he died.

The Powder Mills
Dartmoor, 1873

Built for explosions
—a roof light as a crust of lichen,
walls like bastions.

Made to shed
their hobnails at the door, the men
enter "shod

like parsons". Brimstone
in the air, and the fine black dust
a narrow sun-

slant might reveal
ascending round their heads, a bright host.
Rumbling of the wheels.

Yet Silas who would down
his day's victuals at one sitting "lest
I perish before noon"

never missed a day
"for it minds me of God's mercy. And besides
the work is dry."

A thump in the air,
less heard than felt. They pause. Outside
the pot-bellied mortar

fumes. An overseer
gauges the proving-shot's trajectory. Two score
yards, the powder

[60]

is approved. A rabbit's
white scut jiggles through the gorse, and fear
keeps within limits,

knows its place.
It is another century. Larks shrill and rise,
rise to the emptiness of space.

Night-Offering

It was an afterwards, a cindered waste.
Dim skylines crumbling into dusk.
Torn webs of girders. Soft
as snow, in the dead calm, drifts
of ash, a flat sour aftertaste . . .

Do you hear me? Half in your own dream
you stir beside me. Listen . . . There
were the survivors, shrunk round a thin flame,
hands cradling the glow. What more
to say? I crept near. One of them,

you, turned towards me, lifting from the fire
this fragment that comes with me as I wake
to ordinary dark: a twig of blackthorn, bare,
barbed, angular. The palest foam
of blossom breaks along its ragged wire.